Hen's pens

Russell Punter
Adapted from a story by Phil Roxbee Cox
Illustrated by Stephen Cartwright

Designed by Helen Cooke
Edited by Jenny Tyler and Lesley Sims
Reading consultants: Alison Kelly and Anne Washtell

There is a little yellow duck to find on every page.

Hen settles down on
a tall pile of straw.

With her ten shiny pens,
she is all set to draw.

"Hi Hen," say her friends.
"May we watch what you do?"

Hen's pens sketch fast.
Next she draws tiny Chick.

Then she tries wavy lines.
Some are thin. Some are thick.

Down she hops to the ground,
to draw lines that are long.

But she runs out of paper...

Now I can't carry on!

Hen looks all around.
Has she found what she needs?

She spots lots of eggs.
"I can blob dots on these!"

"That's enough spots and dots,
I like zig-zags the best."

Soon no bird's egg is safe
as she swoops on each nest.

But now whose egg is whose?
It's much harder to tell.

"I'm confused," hisses Snake.
"I left eggs here as well."

They hear five tiny cracks,
from a haystack nearby.

Ahh, it's Snake's stripey babies...
"Hello Ma!" they all cry.

Puzzles

Puzzle 1
Which animal did Hen draw?

1. Cow   2. Snake   3. Chick   4. Pup

Puzzle 2
One word is wrong in this speech bubble. What should it say?

Now I can't hurry on!

Puzzle 3
Spot the six differences between the two pictures.

Puzzle 4
Look at the picture. Are the sentences true or false?

1. One egg has stripes.

2. One egg has spots.

3. Hen's pen is blue.

4. Hen's beak is red.

Answers to puzzles

Puzzle 1

3. Hen drew Chick.

Puzzle 2

Now I can't <u>carry</u> on!

Puzzle 3

Puzzle 4

1. False. One egg does not have stripes.

2. True. One egg has spots.

3. True. Hen's pen is blue.

4. False. Hen's beak is not red.

About phonics

Phonics is a method of teaching reading used extensively in today's schools. At its heart is an emphasis on identifying the *sounds* of letters, or combinations of letters, that are then put together to make words. These sounds are known as phonemes.

Starting to read

Learning to read is an important milestone for any child. The process can begin well before children start to learn letters and put them together to read words. The sooner children can discover books and enjoy stories and language, the better they will be prepared for reading themselves, first with the help of an adult and then independently.

You can find out more about phonics on the Usborne Very First Reading website, **usborne.com/veryfirstreading** (US readers go to **veryfirstreading.com**). Click on the **Parents** tab at the top of the page, then scroll down and click on **About synthetic phonics**.

Phonemic awareness

An important early stage in pre-reading and early reading is developing phonemic awareness: that is, listening out for the sounds within words. Rhymes, rhyming stories and alliteration are excellent ways of encouraging phonemic awareness.

In this story, your child will soon identify the *e* sound, as in **hen** and **pen**. Look out, too, for rhymes such as **draw** – **straw** and **chick** – **thick**.

Hearing your child read

If your child is reading a story to you, don't rush to correct mistakes, but be ready to prompt or guide if he or she is struggling. Above all, give plenty of praise and encouragement.

This edition first published in 2020 by Usborne Publishing Ltd., Usborne House, 83-85 Saffron Hill, London EC1N 8RT, England. usborne.com Copyright © 2020, 2006, 2001 Usborne Publishing Ltd.